Chewie And The Porgs

WRITTEN BY **Kevin Shinick**

ILLUSTRATED BY **Fiona Hsieh**

Disney

LUCASFILM

PRESS

LOS ANGELES · NEW YORK

For Maisy. "You've taken your first step into a larger world." –K. S.

For my parents. –F. H.

The illustrations in this book were rendered in acrylic and oil paint

with special effects added in Adobe Photoshop.

Designed by Scott Piehl

© & TM 2017 Lucasfilm Ltd. All rights reserved.

Published by Disney · Lucasfilm Press,

an imprint of Disney Book Group. No part of this book may be reproduced or

transmitted in any form or by any means, electronic

or mechanical, including photocopying, recording, or by any information storage

and retrieval system, without written

permission from the publisher.

For information address Disney · Lucasfilm Press,

1101 Flower Street, Glendale, California 91201.

Printed in the United States of America

First Edition, December 2017 10 9 8 7 6 5 4 3 2

Library of Congress Control Number on file

FAC-034274-17005

ISBN 978-1-4847-8076-3

Visit the official *Star Wars* website at:

www.starwars.com.

A long time ago in a galaxy far, far away. . . .

There was a planet so distant and so mysterious, it was said to have been hidden among the stars.

The planet is called Ahch-To.

And on this planet stands the very first Jedi temple.

Not many know of its existence . . .
mostly just the Caretakers of the island.

(And now you, of course.)

The only other being with knowledge of this
mystical place is the man who crossed
an entire galaxy to find it . . .

Luke Skywalker,
last of the Jedi Knights.

But this is *not* his story.

This is the story of the porgs,
sweet and lovable creatures that
inhabit Ahch-To Island.

The porgs have lived in peace and tranquility
on the island for many years. Their sanctuary
has remained undisturbed by anyone.

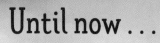

Until now . . .

FRRRROOOOOOOOO

EEP!!!

The *Millennium Falcon* has arrived!

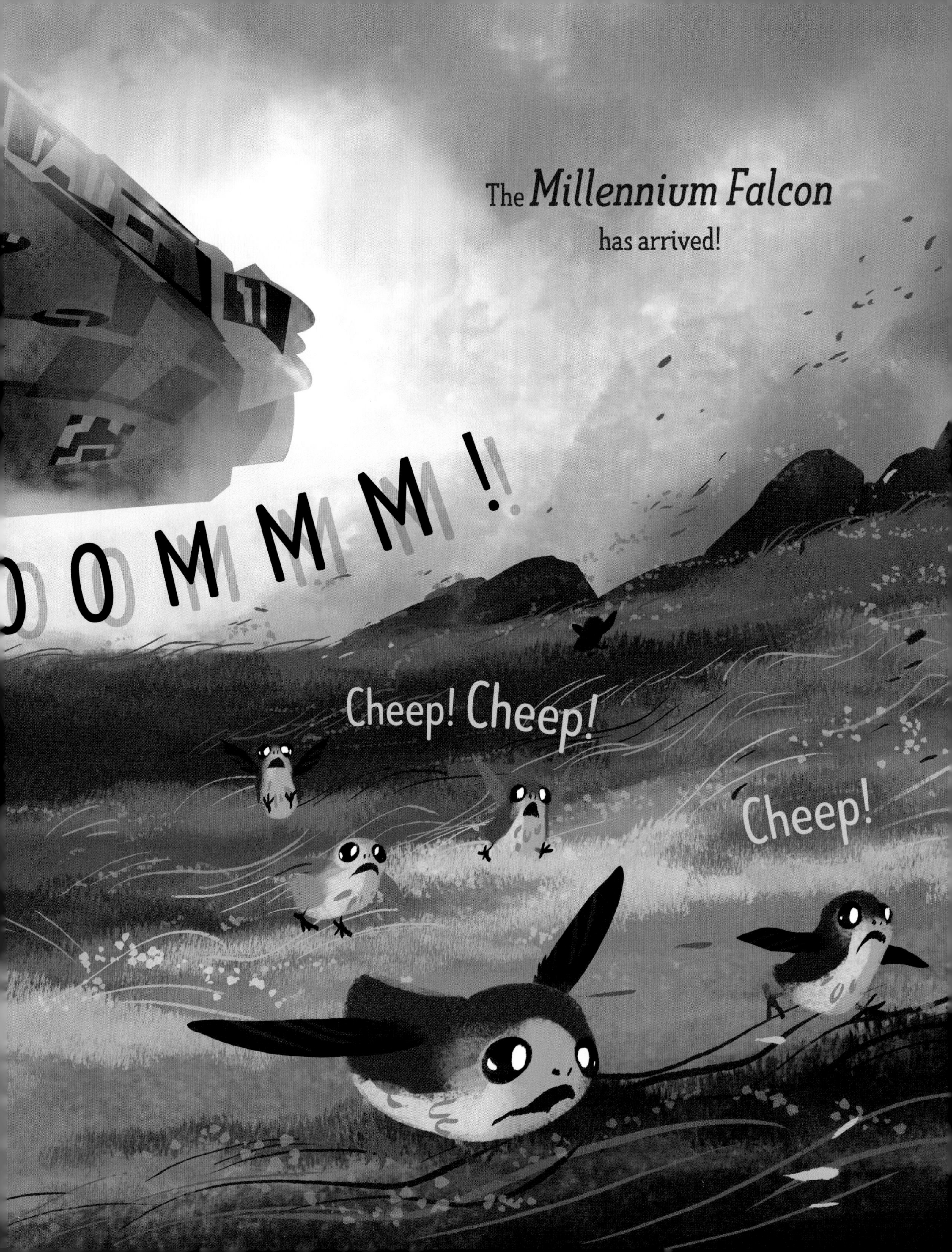

One of the beings who exits the
ship is covered in fur and unlike
anything the porgs have
ever seen before.

The young girl tells the furry one to stay with the ship.
The porgs overhear her refer to him as chewy.

They wonder if this means he is her food. They hope so,
for they are very hungry and he appears to be bite-size.

This will take some investigating.

Back inside the *Millennium Falcon*,
the furry one, Chewbacca the Wookiee,
and R2-D2, a small droid,
are preparing the ship for
the girl's return.

Woop! Woop!

Woop! Woop!

Suddenly, the *Falcon's*
scanners detect
nearby intruders.
Could it be mynocks?
Probe droids?

Chewie goes to check
out the situation.

Lucky for the porgs, their
camouflaging abilities
serve them well.

But Chewie isn't fooled for long.

(And he definitely *isn't* bite-size.)

One porg isn't afraid
of a Wookiee's roar . . .

SCREEEEE!

GRUMBLE!
GRUMBLE!

but he *is* afraid of a Wookiee's grumbling stomach!

Wookiee Fun Fact #17:
Wookiees are always hungry.

But poor Chewbacca
has nothing to eat.

The next day, Chewbacca sets out to find some food.
Chewie is an excellent shot . . .

cheep?

but certain uninvited guests
make concentrating
difficult.

He tries to search
for berries,
but all he finds are
Ahch-Tonian grubs.

Wookiee Fun Fact #35:
Turns out Wookiees hate
Ahch-Tonian grubs.

Chewie thinks back
to the time when
Ewoks devised a trap
to capture him and
his friends.

He decides to build
a trap of his own.

This is *not* what
Chewie intended.

Cheep?

Next, Chewie tries his hand at fishing. He decides to use the disgusting grubs as bait . . . but doesn't get a nibble.

Perhaps he should use more bait? Never mind.

Better luck next time, **Chewbacca.**

Chewie then decides
to ask the locals for help,
but he learns that
fishing season is over
and all the
fish are gone.

While Chewie is away,
the porgs decide to do a little
exploring of their own.

Boo-
bweep?

The porgs have never seen so many
flashing lights and shiny buttons before.

Che-cheep?

Still as hungry as ever,
Chewie returns to the ship
only to find . . .

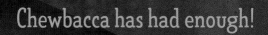

Chewbacca has had enough!

ROOOAR!

Eep! Eep!

Eeeep!

Cheep! Eep!

There must be food *somewhere* on the ship.
Chewie desperately searches all the compartments until...

Success!

Chewie looks around
to make sure
the coast is clear.

And when it is . . .
he gets ready to eat.

Wookiee Fun Fact #77:
Nothing tastes better than
warmly toasted Blue Puff . . .

...Cubes!

Uh-oh. Chewbacca is not going
to be happy about this.

Poor Chewie! He just can't take it anymore.

Eeeep!

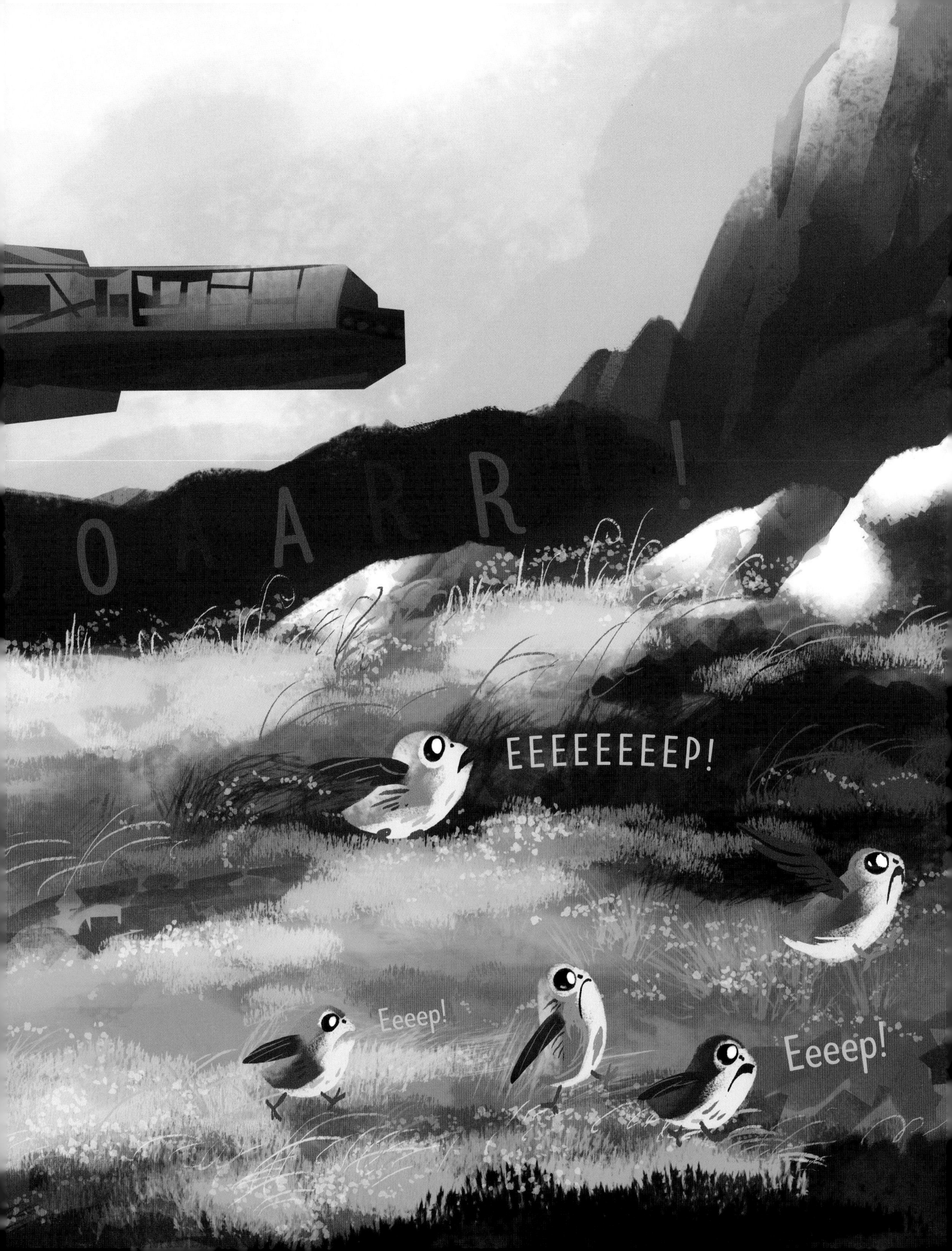

OARR!
EEEEEEEEP!
Eeeep!
Eeeep!

Then Chewie notices something.

One of the *Millennium Falcon*'s landing struts came down on the porgs' nest, crushing the food they stored for winter.

No wonder they've been bothering him so much.

Chewie gets an idea. He uses the *Millennium Falcon*'s sensors to scan the entire island.

And when he finds what he was looking for,
he calls to the porgs to follow him.

He leads them to a hidden lake that still contains fish!

Chewie feels much better now that
he understands the situation.

After all,

Wookiee Fun Fact #1:
Wookiees have hearts of gold.

Chewie and the porgs
enjoy their time together.
They laugh, play,
and feast.

Chewie even learns a new
way to play holochess.

But all journeys must
come to an end.

New missions will take us to faraway places
and teach us new things. And on this mission,

Chewie learned a valuable lesson:

There are some beings in this galaxy who arrive
with questions and leave with answers.

And there are those who arrive with nothing . . .

and leave with new friends.

The End